The Adventures of SPARROWBOY

The Adventures of

Aladdin Paperbacks

New York London Toronto Sydney Singa

OWBOY

BRIAN PINKNEY

First Aladdin Paperbacks edition July 2000

Aladdin Paperbacks
An imprint of Simon & Schuster
Children's Publishing Division
1230 Avenue of the Americas
New York, NY 10020

Also available in a Simon & Schuster Books for Young Readers hardcover edition.
10 9 8 7 6 5 4 3 2 1

The Library of Congress has cataloged the hardcover edition as follows:

Pinkney, J. Brian.
The adventures of sparrowboy / by Brian Pinkney.
p. cm.
Summary: After an encounter with a sparrow, Henry finds he is able to fly
just like his favorite comic book hero, Falconman.
ISBN 0-689-81071-7 (hc.)
[1. Flight—Fiction. 2. Cartoons and comics—Fiction.]
I. Title
PZ7.P63347Ad 1997
[E]—dc20 96-19028
ISBN 0-689-83534-5 (Aladdin pbk.)

To Chloe, my little sparrow

Henry the paperboy always read the front page before he started on his route. Then he read the comics.

Sometimes, the headlines got Henry down. "Why does this stuff have to happen?" he asked himself. "If Falconman was here, he'd make things better."

The Adventures of

BY BARNEY NIPKIN

It has come to pass that a mystical falcon possesses the gift to transfer his powers to a mortal. That man is Trooper Mark Steed who becomes . . . Falconman, a superhero sworn to defend the defenseless.

Later, as Henry rode along Thurber Street tossing papers onto porches, a sparrow swooped down and landed in the middle of his path.

"Hey! Get out of my way!" Henry jammed on the brakes and . . .

ZAP!

Henry flew over the handlebars and soared to the sky.

LOOP-DE-LOOP!
"I can fly!" Henry shouted.

IT'S AIR DELIVERY FOR THE NEIGHBORHOOD . . .
"Hey, I can see everything . . .

OH NO! HERE COMES TROUBLE . . .
GRRRR!
Bruno the bully marched up Thurber Street with Wolf. Then Bruno let Wolf go.

HE'S HUNTING THE TWO RASCALS!
WOOF!
RRRRR!!!!
Will and Matt had been bitten once too often.

IN THE NICK OF TIME . . .

ARP!
"Sit, doggie!"

LOOK! A RUNAWAY WAGON!

WHO HAS THE POWER TO HELP?
CHIRP!

"You were almost a sparrow sandwich," Henry said.

MEANWHILE . . . BRUNO WAS STILL UP TO NO GOOD.
"Hey, Dawn! Does your cat have nine lives?"

"Hey, Bruno! Do you???"

THONK!
". . . Have a nice ride!"

WHAT'S THIS? DOUBLE TROUBLE!
"Let's catch that little birdie . . .

. . . and keep him in our laboratory."

"Now you see him, now you don't!" said Henry.

A SAFE SPOT AT LAST . . .
"What's the matter, little sparrow, forget how to use your wings?"

"You'll be out of danger there," Henry said,
"and I can finish delivering my papers."

SECONDS LATER . . . CAT FOOD?

CHIRP!

CHIRRR

IS IT TOO LATE FOR THE SPARROW?
RRRRRRP!!!
"Hang on, little guy!"

"I don't get it. Why can't you fly?"

A CLUE?

ZAP!
WHOOSH!
ZAP!

THERE'S JUST ONE WAY TO FIND OUT!
Together, Henry and the sparrow returned

to the place where they had first collided.

ZAP!

All was quiet along Thurber Street as Henry rode home. Trouble was nowhere to be seen.

And everything felt just a little better.